Loretta

THE TREASURE OF
ASSATEAGUE ISLAND

Assateague Beach

Size: 8 x 10   Inserts: NO   Version # 5

Every good writer needs a good editor, enthusiast, and publicist.
My wife Therese is all of these.

Contact the author at Trafford Publishing.
Any similarity to people living or dead is purely coincidental.

Note for Librarians: A cataloguing record for this book is available from Library and Archives Canada at www.collectionscanada.ca/amicus/index-e.html
ISBN 1-4120-5873-2

TRAFFORD
PUBLISHING

Offices in Canada, USA, Ireland and UK
This book was published *on-demand* in cooperation with Trafford Publishing. On-demand publishing is a unique process and service of making a book available for retail sale to the public taking advantage of on-demand manufacturing and Internet marketing. On-demand publishing includes promotions, retail sales, manufacturing, order fulfilment, accounting and collecting royalties on behalf of the author.

Book sales for North America and international:
Trafford Publishing, 6E–2333 Government St.,
Victoria, BC v8t 4p4 CANADA
phone 250 383 6864 (toll-free 1 888 232 4444)
fax 250 383 6804; email to orders@trafford.com
Book sales in Europe:
Trafford Publishing (uk) Ltd., Enterprise House, Wistaston Road Business Centre,
Wistaston Road, Crewe, Cheshire cw2 7rp UNITED KINGDOM
phone 01270 251 396 (local rate 0845 230 9601)
facsimile 01270 254 983; orders.uk@trafford.com
Order online at:
trafford.com/05-0774

10 9 8 7 6 5

Table of Contents

TREASURE MAP

Eastern Shore of Virginia

Chincoteague Bay

"GUT"

× home

Chincoteague Island

sandhill

Light house

× Assateague Island

Coast Guard Station

×

Blackbeard's Landing

×

Inlet

×

Wallops Island

×

Chincoteague Inlet

Toms Cove

×

Atlantic Ocean

W

N

S

E

THE TREASURE OF ASSATEAGUE ISLAND

by Frank Stringfellow

Frankie (author)
d Stinky

PROLOGUE

"What do you want to do?" Erin said.

"I don't know," Allison answered. "What would you like to do?"

" We have all afternoon until dinnertime."

"Granddaddy," Erin said. "Tell us a story about when you were young."

Granddaddy looked down into those hopeful blue eyes and the clasped hands and he said thoughtfully, "Climb up on my knee."

"Allison," he said. "Sit right here on the floor."

He pointed to the rug before him. Allison scurried to her knees and onto the blue rug. Granddaddy paused for a long, long time as he reflected back to when he was a child, somewhat older than Erin was. "Things are not really so different now as back then." He started his story.

Chapter 1

BLACKBEARD'S TREASURE

The galley drifted all night at the mercy of the wind and the mountainous waves. Gales of up to one hundred miles an hour had torn away the last of the sails, shreds of which blown by the wind flapped aimlessly from the cross pieces.

The ship's rudder wandered as it drifted toward the shore. The wheel spun aimlessly. What crew remained stared helplessly from the deck as the galley slowly foundered toward the beach. The ship listed consistently before the wind as she dug sideways into the bottom sand. The combers broke violently over the railings sweeping crew and cargo from the deck into the boiling surf. The few remaining crew were drowned immediately completely at the mercy of the elements.

The ship began to break up; and as she did, she inched in towards the beach until her aft section stuck permanently in the sand. The northeaster blew more fiercely now; and the waves continued to work the ship deeper into the sand.

The next day, about noon, there came a break in the clouds and the winds began to subside until at just before dusk a smooth ocean lapped at the aft end of the galley. It appeared to be out of place on the island in the setting sun. It was the summer of 1503.

Many summers and storms passed and gradually with time the sands shifted. The

ship became a part of the beach and sand began to gather about her timbers now slowly rotting.

A hundred years and then about two hundred and the ship was no longer visible. Its only sign of having once existed was a sand hill about twenty feet high where it was once wrecked.

Over the years, the island gradually shifted to the north caused by wind and waves, so that the mound was a few miles inland and more towards the center of the island. It was south of where Assateague lighthouse is today. Beach grass and heather covered it anchoring the sand in place. Pitch pines began to grow on the mound and the surrounding area. A fire started by lightning later on swept it clean of all vegetation except for a single pine tree on the top of the hill. It and only the irrepressible heather and beach grass remained. That part of the island south of where the ship had beached broke through in a hurricane forming Chincoteague Inlet.

Edward Teach, better known as Blackbeard the Pirate, had sailed along the coast of Virginia many times. He had run away to sea when he was in his teens; and after a stint with a privateering expedition, he became a pirate. He was six feet four in height and weighed in at two hundred and thirty-five pounds. He had a long black beard, which extended to his waist and a booming bass voice, which seemed to erupt from somewhere inside the beard like a volcano. He was malicious and violent and a man totally without conscience. He, like all of his crew, rarely washed except when they were forced to by wading in the water.

This spring day in 1718 was calm with only a hint of a wind blowing in from off shore. There was a clear blue sky punctuated by only a few puffs of clouds. The dingy rode up and down in a lazy gentle motion as long swells moved past it on their way to shore. Blackbeard sat in the stern of the dinghy steering with an oar placed in the sculling lock. Six crewmen rowed rhythmically almost as if they were keeping time to the tune of the waves. The mate called cadence in the bow to keep them rowing in unison. They were now two hundred yards off shore; and now, you could hear the waves breaking on the beach in front of them. The boat rode lower in the water than usual and the bow hung out of the water as each swell passed on by. In front of Blackbeard was a small chest of wrought iron that weighed in at about 100 pounds. Inside was booty from the many ships that he had raided along the east coast. The combined weight of the chest and its contents was about 300 pounds.

The Queen Anne's Revenge, his ship, lay at anchor about 700 yards off shore. She was larger than most sailing ships of her time and hardly seemed to rock with the seas.

The dinghy now began to ship water over the sides as they approached the beach because the waves were forming to break on shore. However, they did not break until they were close to shore. First there was a dull bump, then a pause, followed by another bump, then another, and another in more rapid succession as the deepest part of the keel touched the bottom with the forward motion of the boat and the weight of the chest in the rear.

"Weigh oars!" Blackbeard blasted.

The crew gave one last pull and shipped their oars onto the railings and the boat shot forward as if nudged by some unseen hand from behind into the sand ten yards off shore. She came to an abrupt halt causing everyone in the boat to lurch forward. The waves now began to break over the stern of the boat and the crew quickly scrambled over the side and began to guide the boat with the help of the waves onto the beach. The mate tugged hard at the rope fastened to the bow to keep it moving up and forward. The boat suddenly came to a halt again on the hard beach sand.

Blackbeard got up, stepped over the chest and each of the three seats walking to the bow. He then jumped out of the boat and walked on up the hard brown beach to the soft white sand at its crest. The boat lurched forward again; and this time, it finally dug into the beach sand at the surf line.

Four crewmen clamored into the boat from the surf and scampered to the rear of the boat where each of them took hold of the leather thongs at each corner of the chest. Gradually, with effort they carried it over the seats, placed it on the tapered bow, lifted it over the side of the boat and carried it up to the soft beach sand following Blackbeard's footprints. The other three men pulled the boat further up onto the hard beach sand and followed them. The tide was receding so that there was no need to anchor the boat.

Blackbeard surveyed the island. He had seen it from a distance at sea many times; but he had never landed here before. A soft gentle breeze blew his rough brown coat and his red balloon breeches. He wore a wide brimmed hat that would catch the wind and bend sharply to it. He looked inland as the crew brought the chest to the crest of the beach.

Actually, the "crew" consisted of three men including Blackbeard and the other four were prisoners who had been captured during one of his latest raids and saved expressively for this purpose. They had been told that they would be left behind on the island when they were through burying the chest of valuables.

Blackbeard squinted and motioned for them to follow him for he knew exactly where he wanted to go. Before he had dropped anchor offshore, he had spotted a tall pine tree on a mound of sand from the sea that made it stand out from all of the surrounding terrain. They carried the chest in shifts rotating arms every few minutes. Eventually, they crossed the two hundred yards of beach, primary and secondary dunes, and moved into the scrub brush. They waded through the shallow swamps over into the cool of the pine forests. Now, the going was faster. They carried the chest two hundred more yards inland until they came to the base of a sandy hill.

On top of the hill was an old pitch pine tree about three feet in diameter and at least seventy-five feet tall. Its bark resembled alligator hide. It was much older than the surrounding trees because it had been the only tree to survive a forest fire started by lightning over a hundred years ago. Its canopy had a wind swept look because of the constant exposure to the winds sweeping the island.

"Dig!" said Blackbeard, and the four men began to dig in earnest two at a time with relief every five minutes. The ground was sandy and it was hard for Blackbeard to walk up the hill to its top where the tree was. His huge black boots made the trip even harder; for it seemed that for every three steps he took forward, he seemed to go back one. At the top, he could see the masts of the Queen Anne's Revenge hardly moving at all. He could not see the dinghy because it was hidden from view by the crest of the white beach sand.

"Captain!" Blackbeard heard; but he took no notice of the mate.

The mate knew better than to call him again and disturb his train of thought. He looked almost royal as he stood there gazing out to sea, very much as if he were composing a sonnet. Yet, there was hardness, a meanness that came over his face upon closer inspection.

He turned abruptly and walked purposefully down the hill to where the two men were still digging the hole. Only their heads and shoulders could be seen when they stood up straight. The hole was about five feet deep and equally as wide. Water was beginning to seep into it and covered the bottom.

He walked over to the hole and looked down. Suddenly, in the flash of an eye he withdrew his brace of two pistols and shot each man resting at the edge of the hole in the head. In equal fashion he took out his sword and with two smooth strokes cut off the head of one man in the hole . He then smashed the head of the other man with a tremendous blow of his sword as he tried to duck down. A cold wind began to blow softly. One could feel the island begin to shiver and groan in agony. It was as if it could sense the horror that had taken place. Blackbeard had kept his promise and left them behind on the island.

15

The mate and the other crewman quickly moved to the chest and dragged it over the sand to the edge of the hole. The two of them jumped into the hole. They tilted the chest and it slid into the hole with a thump. There was barely enough room for the two men to get on top of the chest and climb back out. Five minutes later the sand was back in the hole and the area was re-covered with a scattering of pine shats and a few pine cones. Each man broke off a pine bough and dragged it behind him as they retraced their steps back to the dinghy behind Blackbeard.

Periodically, Blackbeard would look back to take a bearing and fix the spot in his memory. When they reached the beach crest, the men dragged the dinghy off of the beach into the surf. Blackbeard stopped at the top to take one last look back from the beach. Then, without notice he turned and strode purposefully across the beach sand, swung his left leg over the side of the dingy, sat on the rail while he pulled his right leg into the boat. The two men now pushed the dinghy out and hopped aboard and assumed their places before Blackbeard had placed the steering oar into the sculling lock.

It took longer to row the boat back to the ship for there were only two oarsmen. The mate was silent now for there was no need to coordinate the rowing. All that could be heard was the rhythmic swish, swish, swish of the bow parting each wave to the stroke of the oars. The sound of the waves breaking onto the beach gradually faded off into the distance.

Chapter 2

FRANKIE AND SKIP

It was hot and humid. Sultry was the word which best described the day. The salt just clung to the skin as the water evaporated away. Frankie had nothing to do. It was summer and school was out. Everyday was pretty much like the day before and presumably like each day to come, he thought. He sat on the dock with his bare feet dangling a few feet above the water's surface.

He squinted his blue eyes that reflected the light from the surface of the water as he looked off into the distance. He could see the faint movement of a man chest deep in the water on the other side of the marsh. He was wading clams. Periodically, he would bend slightly to pick the clams from between his toes and toss them into the boat beside him. He would do this never ending routine for a lifetime as his father had done and his father before him.

The boy shifted on his buttocks; then suddenly, he slapped at his fair skinned arm. That horsefly was pestering him again, he thought, as he scratched at the bite. His nails left behind a series of white lines in the salt on his skin. There must be a reason for horseflies, he thought. They are probably here to pester man.

He tossed his head causing his sandy hair to shift to one side. The smell of creosote from the pilings filled his nose and still burned his lips from the morning's swim. He looked down and could see it slowly seeping V-like from the pilings in a spectrum of colors as the current carried it away. He was twelve years old and would be going into the sixth grade this year.

He wondered what he would do in life? Perhaps he would dig clams like that fisherman out there. He wasn't afraid, he thought. He hoped that it would be exciting. He had lived on the island all of his life. He loved it. He didn't know about anywhere else.

He stood up one leg at a time stretching out all thin but muscular five foot three inches of him. His shoulders were reddened over the bronze tan from having been out in the sun too long. He was as brown as a berry to his waistline. He only wore a pair of faded blue jeans. His life was so simple. He rarely washed because he swam every day and he rarely wore underwear.

Why on earth would anyone wear underwear, he thought?

It just cut you and made you hotter. He walked lightly onto the oyster shells that filled the dock as if he were walking across water. No one could see the calluses on the soles of his feet which were re-grown each summer by walking on the shells and building them up.

He made his way over to an area where fresh shells had been applied as dock fill. They smelled of rotting oyster flesh and crawled with flies. He bent over and expertly picked out a good one and fit it in the groove between his thumb and forefinger. He leaned back on his right foot, and raising his left leg, threw it on its way across the creek into the marsh on the other side.

The creek, also more accurately called "the gut", was a waterway about four hundred yards long and about 20-40 yards wide in places which connected Chincoteague Channel with Chincoteague Bay. Frankie lived on the creek but he swam in "the gut".

Not bad, he thought. I wish I could fly.

He was one reason that they were always putting new shells on the dock, he thought.

He felt a tinge of guilt at first; and the back of his neck got redder than it already was because if the owner of the dock caught you throwing away his shells, he was sure to yell and curse at you.

But, it was worth it, he thought. There must be a ton of shells over there on the marsh from throwing and skipping oyster shells over the water.

Skip was his best friend and next door neighbor. He was a little older than Frankie, somewhat shorter; but in most respects, they looked about the same. They were inseparable friends; but today, Skip was visiting his grandmother at the south end of the island. He would return that evening for tomorrow's trip to Assateague the outer barrier island. Frankie had invited Skip to come along.

The boy walked across the dock to where the boat was moored in a slip. It was 16 feet long and six feet across and clinker built; e.g. it had overlapping boards. It was a seaworthy craft with oaken rails and painted white outside above the copper paint. The inside was painted green. She was high off of the water with three seats. One was forward and the others were aft and in the middle of the boat.

The 16 horsepower Johnson outboard motor could be steered from the rear seat. Gosh but that engine was temperamental, he thought. Only he could run it. He always took a tool chest with him in case the engine broke down.

His father had said he thought that it discouraged the engine from breaking down.

He saw that she was dry inside as she bobbed up and down to the lop, lop, lop sounds of the waves pushing against the boat. Occasionally the ropes would moan when there was more than usual strain on them. He had to squint again because the white paint reflected the sun off of the water into his eyes.

A better boat was never built, he thought.

"Frankie!" his aunt called. "Lunch!"

"Coming!" he yelled back; and with that he walked gingerly across the shells and cinders into the house.

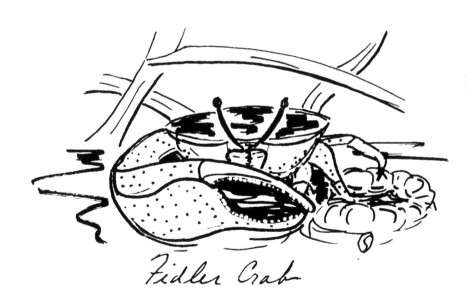

Fidler Crab

Cockle

Chapter 3

CHINCOTEAGUE, ASSATEAGUE,
A WAY OF LIFE

Frankie lived on the island of Chincoteague, Virginia. It was a fishing village of about 4-5,000 people that lay about ten miles off of the East Coast of the United States.

The island had three main sources of income in addition to local merchants: raising chickens, fishing, and a shirt factory. He had worked in a chicken house once but he didn't like that. The dry smell of mash and the vigilant job of collecting dead chickens made him sick. He had seen the men go to sea; and although he was too young to go himself, he saw that it was exciting but hard and dangerous work with low pay. He had only passed by the shirt factory but he had never been inside. There was an air of mystery about it because it had no windows. No one could see out. No one could see inside. He had heard that it was nothing more than a sweatshop. Besides that, they only hired women. It all seemed to be very dull and boring except for fishing.

The island was about seven miles long and less than a few miles wide. It was part of a system of barrier islands and beaches that extended along the Eastern Shore peninsula. Seaward of Chincoteague was Assateague Island. It was about 37 miles long and a few hundred yards wide to over a mile wide in places. Its sands were constantly shifting. An inlet called Chincoteague Inlet separated Assateague from Wallops Island that lay south of it.

It was unpopulated except for horses that lived off of the marsh grasses. Legend had it they swam ashore from a Spanish galleon that had wrecked just off shore during a storm during the 16th century. Probably, they were introduced from the mainland and just remained there.

Frankie had come to the island when he was five years old with his father, his aunt, and his cousin, Sammy, who lived with them most of his life. His father ran a bus line that covered the southern part of the Eastern Shore.

They lived better than most of the other people who lived on the creek; but they were not rich. They had the only indoor toilet facility with a bathtub in the neighborhood. Neighbors would ask to take a bath, a luxury at that time.

He lived in a strange world; for in some respects, the area was 20 years behind the rest of the United States; yet in other respects, it was 20 years ahead of the rest of the country. The Chesapeake Bay Bridge and the Chesapeake Bay Bridge Tunnel had not yet been built; and the bridge connecting Chincoteague to Assateague had also not been built. The boy lived the best of both the past and the future in the present. He didn't know this then; yet there was an inkling of it in the back of his mind.

Wallops Island was south of both islands. It had a missile base on it run by a civilian agency of the government; and just out of his back window he could see the Chincoteague Naval Air Station.

Many times he and his cousin would drop anchor off of Wallops Island and watch the jets from the base bomb and strafe the section of the island where the target area was. They did this often when they were fishing. It filled in the slack times. Sometimes a sounding rocket would be launched from the island to sample and measure conditions in the upper atmosphere. So, there was always something to do or to be seen during the summers.

Science is so exciting, he thought.

Assateague Pony

Bony Fish

Chapter 4

GOING FISHING

It was six o'clock the next morning. Skip had been up since 5:30, dressed, and he had come over for breakfast. His aunt was up early because his father got up by four o'clock to go to work on the mainland. "Going fishing today, huh?" his father said.

"Off Wallops," Frankie replied.

"See you this evening then, Tomcat," his father said rubbing his son's head; then he put on his gray hat and walked out of the door. I sure wish I was a kid again, he thought, as he started the car. They could hear the car fade off into the distance.

Skip said nothing up until now because his mouth was too full of pancakes and bacon. After breakfast, Skip and Frankie walked on out to the wash house and started loading supplies from it into the boat. First, they put the engine on the transom. That took both of them to do it. Skip stood beside the engine on the dock holding it upright while Frankie got into the boat. Frankie then reached up and in one smooth motion he lowered it into the boat and onto the transom. Skip then handed Frankie the toolbox, oars, the gas tank, the crab net, and the fishing tackle followed by lunch, a gallon of water, and the bait. Squid was the bait. Skip loaded the life preservers and the rest of the supplies while Frankie hooked up the gasoline tank.

Today would be fun, Frankie thought.

His aunt came out of the house to see them off. She had a worried expression on her face as she said, "Be careful!" She always said that; but she always let them go too.

Skip untied the lines both fore and aft and pushed the boat stern first out of the slip with his foot then he jumped into the stern of the boat. The stern turned slowly downstream as the current caught her. Frankie checked the balance of the boat and saw Skip assuming his position in the bow. He primed the engine, advanced the throttle to start, and pulled the engine over. It coughed and sputtered. He pulled again and the same thing happened. He pulled again and now the engine caught. He rapidly throttled the engine back. A gray plume of smoke rose from the water behind the transom. It smelled of burned oil.

Frankie shifted the gearshift from neutral to forward and the boat began to move slowly against the current. They made their way along the creek slowly so as not to cause waves which would cause the boats which were docked, to bang excessively against the pilings. As they left the mouth of the creek, Frankie advanced the throttle and the bow rose out of the water as the speed picked up and the boat settled onto a plane.

The wind blew in their faces and the boats parked along the docks were rapidly left behind. Frankie now moved the throttle wide open and the engine ran with an even hum as the boat planed out leaving only a slight wake trailing behind in a long V. She was moving at 17 mph. The boys could not speak to one another because of the engine noise. Frankie could easily see past Skip whose brown hair was blowing wildly in the wind. Skip was barefoot with both feet tucked up under him and his right hand held the bow rope. As the bow rose up and down to the rhythm of the waves, he bounced accordingly. He wore a white T-shirt and faded blue jeans.

The day was clear with hardly a wind; but it was not hot and the wind and spray felt good on the face. The smells of the marsh filled the nose as they swiftly ran half the length of the island. There was nothing to do but to be aware, steer, and throw the mind into daydreams to pass the time away.

Frankie could see a seagull gliding leisurely beside the boat above him and to his right. Occasionally it would flap its wings. Frankie wished that he could fly like the gull.

He could see himself in his minds eye flying a jet. Roaring in over the landscape and strafing a target, pulling back on the stick, feeling the downward pull of gravity as the earth in front of him gave way to sky. He could feel the rapid shot forwards as he cut in the after burners and put the airplane into a series of rolls as he screwed his way up into the clear blue sky and then arched over in a long slow loop and repeated the maneuver over and over again.

Skip stared off to the horizon. He could see himself as captain of his own trawler and handling the wheel in a violent storm with waves crashing over the wheelhouse. He could picture himself bringing her and the crew back in intact repeating this day in and day out. These were boys with imagination who never tired of their dreams. Speed and danger had an allure all of its own.

The boat passed beyond the tip of the island and into the narrow inlet separating it from Wallops Island. Frankie throttled the engine back now and gradually brought the boat around so that she was facing west. He then cut the engine and the boat glided forward to the lop, lop, lop of the waves slapping at the bottom of the boat. Skip threw the anchor overboard just when the forward motion of the boat had slowed and it had started moving backwards with the current. The rope played out suddenly then stopped as the anchor grabbed the bottom. Skip then gradually played out more slack on the rope assuming an ever-decreasing angle from the vertical until it stopped and moaned from the tension of the boat pulling at the line. The boat then jerked in line with the rope and current and resumed its lop, lop, lop to the rhythm of the waves.

Wallops Island was in the immediate distance to the south. The red roof of the abandoned boat house was clearly visible tucked into the dark green trees which dominated the landscape. The marsh covered a broad expanse between the boat and the boathouse; and the target area was to the interior of the island. The stern of the boat pointed in the direction of the fast flowing inlet, which cut between Wallops Island and Chincoteague. It led into Toms Cove, an expansive bay between Chincoteague and Assateague. Only the green marsh could be seen to the West. Sometimes the cry of the rail could be heard. The tide was slowing in its recession. It was a good time to fish. The two boys had timed their arrival so that they could begin fishing just before low slack tide.

"Well, let's bait up," Frankie said.

Skip had already taken the squid out from under the bow where the lunch and water were also stored. He had already opened the package and cut it into long thin strips with a Boy Scout knife and lay them on the bait board. Frankie took a few strips of it and double hooked a strip onto the top hook. He did the same thing with the bottom hook. They were bottom rigged to catch flounder.

Skip was the first one to lower his rig over the side and it slid through the water and disappeared on its way to the bottom. Frankie's rig soon followed. After a while there was a tug at the line and Skip pulled at the line sinking the hook home. The flounder swam wildly with the line as Skip gave it slack line to play it in order to wear it out. Finally, the flounder was brought to the surface swimming almost willingly like a pet coming to its master. He lifted it over the side and into the boat and the hook was removed with a pair of pliers. Skip threw it into the ice chest. It weighed about a pound and would make a meal after it was filleted. The boys rarely talked when they fished; for they had been told that the fish would hear them and would not come near the boat.

Frankie stared off towards Wallops Island. He could hear the cheers as he threw the ball. He sure would like to play major league ball, he thought. He would strike the batter out in the last of the ninth inning and save the game.

Suddenly, there was a violent tug at his line. The string was jerked from his hands as if he had hooked a truck. Frankie sat upright and his mind jerked back to reality. The line now played out as it ran back and forth across the water in front of him. He reached out and grabbed it but it just kept going.

"What is it?" Skip said.

"I don't know, but it sure is big."

He brought the line slowly into the boat with effort and just when the fish was near the surface, it would dive with a series of charging tugs and pull most of the line with it. But, less line was played out each time. Finally, as the fish came into view this time, Frankie could see the broad bluish body and the wide set malevolent eyes staring back at him.

"A sting ray, pass me the knife." The ray rolled over and over showing its white belly as it lashed out again and again at Frankie with its tail.

"Stay clear of the tail!" Skip cautioned.

The ray had a poisonous spine on its dorsal surface and could inflict an extremely painful and sometimes fatal wound. Frankie reached over the rail carefully and cut the line. The ray stopped moving when the tension was released from the line; and looking Frankie directly in the eye, slowly sank beneath the surface of the water and disappeared into the depths below.

Frankie then went about the business of preparing a new rig in order to resume fishing. The morning passed fast as each boy caught seven flounders ranging from one to three pounds. The remainder of the time was spent catching "trash fish" and innumerable crabs. All of these fish were thrown back into the water.

By now it was eleven o'clock and the tide was coming in. The boat had gradually shifted with the tide. The boys pulled in their fishing lines, washed the slime and smell of the fish and bait from their hands in the salt water.

"Pass the lunch, Skip," Frankie said.

Each boy ate a peanut butter sandwich with jelly while exchanging small talk followed by sips of water from the glass jug. By now, it was warm but it still quenched the thirst.

27

"Too bad that they are not flying today," Skip said.

"Yeah!" Frankie said. "Well, since we've used low slack tide and high slack isn't until 5, let's go over to Assateague and play."

Skip pulled on the anchor rope and the boat began to move slowly forward. The bottom only gave up the anchor with a tug when the rope was at the vertical. Skip washed it in the water before tucking it up under the bow. They drifted with the current for a while towards the distant marsh as they cleaned bait and bottom grass from their hooks and trimmed the boat for traveling. Everything had to be fastened down for the trip through the inlet and across Toms Cove.

The trip across Toms Cove was slower than the trip along the length of the island because of the long swells coming into the inlet from the ocean. The waves were two to three feet high and the boat had to travel at about two-thirds speed. It was windier too but not dangerously so. It was like riding a roller coaster.

The bow would heave out of the water leaving Skip suspended in the air momentarily at the crest of the wave as it fell back into the trough. After the bow hit the next wave, Skip would be thrown into the seat. This bucking up and down was not unlike the bucking of a horse and one could get quite sore from it, particularly, where one sat. Assateague Island was now close.

They beached the boat about a half-mile south of the Coast Guard station where the island hooked into a sandy spit. Frankie throttled the engine back and the bow glided forward and nudged gently onto the sand. Both boys surged forward. It was 12:30 in the afternoon. They saw the red lighthouse far off to the left in the distance.

Skip jumped out onto the hard beach sand and pulled the rope after him. The boat slid forward. Frankie tilted the engine up out of the water and moved forward jumping from the bow onto the sand. He then helped Skip pull the boat as far onto the sand as possible. They dug the anchor deep into the sand. Both boys then looked about them.

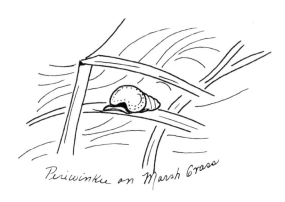

Periwinkle on Marsh Grass

28

Chapter 5

HUNTING FOR SHELLS ON THE BEACH

Conch shells were strewn all over the sand and terns were flying over the beach where their nests were made. The red roof of the Coast Guard station could be seen up the beach a few hundred yards on the cove side a good distance from the forest. The forest was green and lush and wind swept in appearance. Further up the beach beyond the forest one could see the lighthouse. Off of the point looking south were the beaches of Wallops Island interrupted by the launching pads and rocket assembly buildings. The backdrop was green foaming sea breaking on the white beaches, blue sky, and the deep green of the forest pines. The hump of the island sand shielded the sea running off Assateague Beach. They did not take lunch or water because they did not expect to be gone that long. After all, the tide was now coming in.

Both boys set out across the sand with tennis shoes on because they had learned from hard experience that the sand was so hot in the midday sun that it burned blisters even on their tough feet. As they got up on the crest of the beach or soft white sand, the terns dove at them sometimes singularly or in flocks. The boys put their hands on their heads, ducked down, and waved their hats at the birds as they ran across the beach. The terns made their nests on the sand. The young birds were sandy in color so that the boys had to be careful so as not to step on them. The boys often talked about this and Frankie wondered how those tiny birds could survive in the searing heat!

The boys made their way on across the beach until they reached the crest of the white sandy beach. It was always breathtaking when you could first see the breaking ocean surf. You could hear it like the continuous roar you hear when you put a conch shell to your ear. You could smell it before you could see it; and that served to increase the anticipation even more. Frankie and Skip always raced to the crest of the sands to see who would be the first to see it. It was blue-green and seemed to stretch forever to the east. It was hard to believe that the next land was 3,000 miles way over there beyond the horizon and across the Atlantic Ocean. The wind was blowing out of the east to shore. The white foaming water crashed in succession onto the hard, gray, beach sand. There always were shells being moved up and down the beachfront by the waves.

The boys paused for about five minutes then they began the inevitable walk up the beach. There was no one on the beach so it was like being on a deserted island. Little sandpipers skittered along the edge of the surf moving up and down the beach sand in rhythm with the breaking waves. Willets flew with white, flashing wings skimming the waves. They dug for mole crabs and other crustaceans exposed against the sand washed off by the receding waves.

Frankie always liked to walk in the surf and feel the "undertow" of the receding waves washing through his toes. But if they were to find some pretty shells, they had to walk along the upper hard beach sand along the debris line. As they walked along, they found red scallops shells that resembled fans and fresh whelks with their smooth beautifully colored nacre. Each one seemed more beautiful than the previous one. It was hard to decide which ones to keep; so, they kept them all! They deposited their brown paper bags on the sand as they filled up. They would pick them up later on the way back to the boat.

The boys had walked 3-4 miles up the beach and were getting tired of collecting shells. It was 2 o'clock in the afternoon now and they would have to turn back soon.

whelk

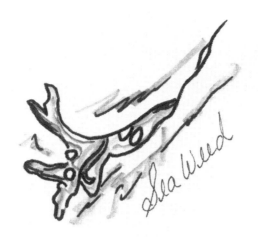

Chapter 6

FINDING THE TREASURE

"Let's go over to the pines," Skip said. "We'll rest for a while where it is cool."

The boys made their way across the wide sandy beach, over the primary and secondary dunes onto a low sandy area to the cool pine forest. Pine shats covered the floor making it soft along with the sand. The forest surrounded a sand hill 30-40 feet high. The boys thought it would be fun to climb the hill. At the top they could see the sea and the white beach sand and the sand dunes.

Suddenly, Skip pushed Frankie and he rolled head over heels five feet down the hill. The battle was on: "King on the Mountain."

"Why you!" Frankie said as he climbed the hill on all fours.

"King on the Mountain!" Skip chided. At that, Frankie reached out and grabbed Skip by the ankle. He pulled Skip's feet out from under him and down the hill they both rolled.

"Ouch!"

"What's wrong?" Frankie said.

"I hurt my head," he said as he rubbed a bump now rising from a red area on his forehead. I hurt my head on that and he pointed at the corner of an iron box sticking out of the sand.

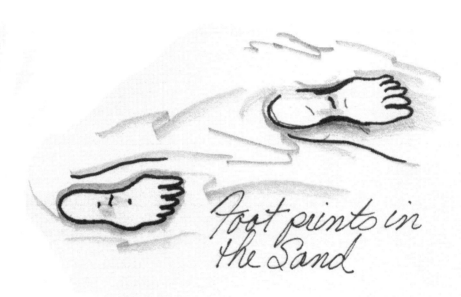

Foot prints in
the Sand

Doubloons

Chapter 7

THE TREASURE

"What's this?" Frankie said and he reached over and touched the box.

It was not wood but rusted iron. He brushed away the shats and sands uncovering more of it. By now Skip was caught up in the enthusiasm of sensing an adventure and he too was on his knees pulling sand away from the box. The boys scrapped sand away for five minutes with their hands and saw that it was two feet wide and three feet long. It was wooden but it was somewhat rotted. It was held together by bands of wrought iron. The iron bands alone kept the chest intact. The lock was centered at the junction of the lid and the main body of the chest. The chest smelled earthy. The boys continued to scrape sand away from all sides of it. They came to the bottom of the chest four feet down. There were rotted leather straps still attached to each corner. Skip bent down at one end and Frankie bent down at the other end. Both of them grabbed the straps and pulled at the same time. The chest did not move. Perhaps if they both pulled at one end! Frankie moved to Skip's end and both of them pulled at the straps. Suddenly, Skip's strap broke from the strain and he fell backwards.

Frankie looked back at Skip and said, "It won't budge. Are you all right?"

Both he and Skip focused at the same time on the two skulls and bones protruding partially hidden by the sand.

"Gosh!" Frankie said. "What is it? It's human! Someone has been killed! My gosh, do you suppose that we have found some old graves?"

"During the last century settlers had lived on Assateaague but hadn't they lived closer to where the lighthouse was?" Skip said.

"I don't know. The person in this box must have been awfully short." Frankie said.

"But why would they bury someone in an iron box? That doesn't make any sense. Do you suppose that we have discovered buried treasure?"

"Try to get the lid open!" Frankie said excitedly.

They kicked at the lid and tried to pry it loose with sticks and branches.

"I'll go get a shell from the beach."

"No you won't!" Skip said. "You're not leaving me here all by myself."

"Well, we can't open it. We can't carry it. It isn't going anyplace either. Even if we could get it out of its hole we could not possibly carry it all that distance back to the boat so, let's cover it back up and come back for it later," Frankie said.

"OK! We can always come back."

The boys refilled the hole containing the chest and covered it over entirely with sand. They covered the skulls with sand and stuck a large leg bone in the sand beside the box to mark it for when they would return. They took notice of the landscape all the way back across the dunes to the beach. From the beach crest they could see a large pine tree on top of the sandy hill.

The boys could not contain themselves because they were so excited. They ran and ran, partly from fear, or guilt that they were intruding where they had no right to be, and partly because they had to release all of that pent-up energy. They forgot their bags of shells. They did not even notice them. They paid no attention to the terns attacking them as they ran back to the boat.

When they reached the beach at the point, they saw that the boat was floating 30 yards off shore. They paused catching their breath for a long time; then Skip got up, took off his shoes and shirt and swam out to the boat. He reached up, grabbed the railing and jumped, pulling himself up onto it in one smooth motion. He stepped into the boat, pulled at the anchor rope and the boat moved forward. He washed the anchor in the water and tucked it up under the bow. He then picked up an oar and poled the boat to the beach.

"We can't tell anyone about this," Frankie said as he stepped into the boat.

It was 5:30 p.m. and the trip home took only a few hours. The wind had died out so the water was calm now. The sun was lower in the sky but there was a long time until sunset. It was noticeably cooler and Skip shivered in the bow from being wet as the wind blew before the speeding boat. He could still see those skulls and bones.

They were blaming him for something, he thought; but he did not know what. He shivered at the thought. Frankie could still see them too; and a shiver ran up his back as he steered the boat beyond the inlet and turned the boat north to begin the trip home along the length of the island.

When they reached home, docked, and had unloaded everything, Frankie said to Skip, "We can't tell anyone about this Skip. See you tomorrow."

Seagulls

Chapter 8

PLANS TO RECOVER THE TREASURE

Skip came onto the dock stripped to his waist. The shells tinkled as he walked gingerly over to where Frankie sat on the dock next to the Rachel, a fishing trawler. He sat beside Frankie but said nothing for a while, and then he spoke, "You know, I think that we had better rethink this whole thing of not telling anyone else. If we go back there to the island, we are not going to be able to carry the treasure no matter what kind of tools we have in getting it out of the hole."

"Who could we tell? Who could we trust to not tell between the time we told them and the time we got back there?" Frankie said.

"We wouldn't have to tell them anything until we got ready to go. We would only have to get them to go there."

"How about Sammy? He's strong and he's here. Let's think about it. What tools will we need?"

"Shovels, pipe for rolling the box over the sand. A wagon would just dig into the sand," Skip said.

"I think that we should beach the boat closer to the pines. We could land north of the Coast Guard station and that would leave us only a few hundred yards to roll and carry the chest," Frankie said.

"Sounds good. Anything else?"

"We'll have to go during the week so our parents won't be able to come," Frankie said.

"Why not tell them? Maybe they would help us."

"Do you really want your parents to come along Skip?" Frankie said with emphasis.

"I guess not," Skip said looking down.

The Rachel's ropes moaned as she pulled at them in a slight gust of wind.

"A hammer! We'll need a hammer to smash the lock open. What will we do if we find a body in the box?" Skip said and he shivered.

"No more than what we would do if we found nothing. We'll just cover everything up and come home. If it's treasure, we'll bring it home. If we can't carry the whole chest then we will carry whatever we can and go back and get the rest later."

" How did it get there?" Frankie wondered aloud.

" I heard that there were pirates who used to bury their treasures on these islands. Maybe one buried it and forgot where; or maybe he was killed after he buried it and no one else knew where he had buried it."

"Maybe. I sure hope that he didn't leave a curse behind. Let's go back tomorrow," Frankie said.

"Sounds good to me. Let's go ask Sammy if he will go."

The two boys got up from where they were sitting on the dock; and talking in low voices to one another, they walked gingerly over the shells back to the house.

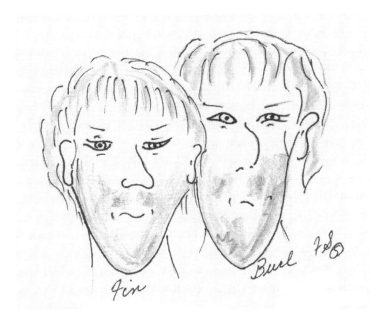

Chapter 9

FIN AND BURL, THE RACHEL

Fin's blood shot eyes watched the two boys as they opened the door to the house and went inside. He was lying in a bunk below by an open porthole in the forward cabin of the Rachel. His feet were dangling over the end. They said that he would do anything for a five-dollar bill hence his name Fin. His brother, Burl was the alter ego of Fin but shorter. They both smoked, cursed, and drank and, of course, fished; but he was an able captain. It was a hard life. He was annoyed at first by the boy's talk; but as he listened, he began to get the drift of their conversation. He had two days growth of beard and his head hurt.

Would this boat ever stop rocking, he thought?

Treasure, he thought, money! He would never have to work again. It would buy a lot of whiskey. He'd show the rest of the people.

They always put me down, he thought.

He reached into his left shirt pocket, took out a cigarette and lit it flipping the lit match out of the porthole. He exhaled gently and thoughtfully. Burl slept on his left side in the opposite bunk with his back to Fin. He snored like a buzz saw. The cabin smelled of gasoline, alcohol, cigarette smoke and more than just a touch of B.O.

Devil's Purse

Shark

Chapter 10

RETURN TO ASSATEAGUE ISLAND

The boys spent the rest of the day assembling tools that they would need to open and move the chest. Sammy had wanted to go over to Assateague; so he was easy to convince. He was much older than the boys were; therefore, the boy's parents just thought nothing unusual of the trip.

Fin had no trouble convincing Burl of all of the possibilities for them if they suddenly came into a large sum of money.

"We could retire for life," Fin said.

On Wednesday, the three boys got up early as usual. They ate, loaded the boat, and were on their way out of "the creek" by seven. They took no notice of the fact that the Rachel was not docked where she usually was. The trip along the length of the island, through the inlet, and into Toms Cove was uneventful.

"Maybe they'll be flying and practicing today," Sammy said.

Frankie figured that this was as good a time as any to tell him the truth; so he throttled the engine back until it cut off and began to slow into a random drift with the current. Both boys explained what they had found on the previous trip and apologized for not telling him the whole truth. They told him that they would put him ashore at the inlet if he did not want to go with them. But, that they were going on anyway.

At first he was angry; but then he thought it would be an adventure to come along.

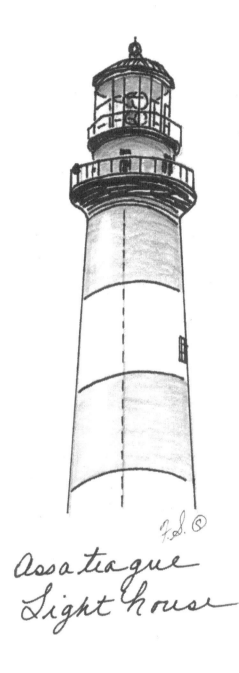

Assateague Light house

Frankie restarted the engine and throttled it up. This time they veered to the left of the marker buoy that marked the channel to Chincoteague Inlet. They did not notice the Rachel drifting with the current in the distance.

Fin was in no hurry for he simply wanted to keep the boys in view from a distance. He increased the speed when he had cleared the shallows and moved the Rachel further out into deeper water. The Rachel sank at the stern because she was not as fast as the boys' boat; but she was fast enough to stay close enough to shadow the fast moving boat in the small bay.

"How many were there?" yelled Fin to Burl.

" I saw three!" he yelled back above the noise of the engines.

The boys gradually turned north and were traveling slower now since they were moving out of the channel and into unfamiliar waters. Frankie steered the boat towards a point about a mile north of the Coast Guard station. There appeared to be a break in the marsh at that point.

As it turned out there was an old abandoned dock there and a crude channel led up to it. The boys did not know that. Fin did. He could see that the boys were headed for the old loading dock. At one time fish were used as fertilizer for crops; so, there was a "fish factory" on the island. These "fish factories" processed "trash fish", bunkers, to fertilizer, which were then shipped to the mainland for use. They were loaded onto boats at the loading dock; but this had been forty years earlier.

Fin slowed the Rachel now and crept to the left of the buoy. He would let them land first and then move in and take the treasure when they had it loaded onto the boat. Let them do all of the work, he thought and he chuckled to himself at the thought.

Sandpipers

Chapter 11

HORSEFLIES, MOSQUITOES, AND GNATS

The boys reached the old loading dock by now. It was just a row of pilings leading to where the hard beach sand began to meet the marsh. The green flies, mosquitoes, and gnats were unbearable. The boys were not near the marsh during the previous trip and there was a sea blown wind; so, they had not even seen a horsefly. This time the breeze was blowing from the marsh; and they were cruising near the marsh. The flies were aggressive. They would fly right into you, ram you wide open on the head, and knock you backward in surprise. It was a wonder that such a small creature could hit so hard.

"This is not worth it. I would not do this again for all the gold in China. Maybe it will be better when we get away from this marsh," Skip said. It wasn't.

Frankie throttled the engine back and it stopped. He raised the lower unit out of the water and the boat slid softly onto the sand with a shush. Skip jumped out followed by Sammy and they pulled the boat further up on the sand. Frankie began to hand each boy food, water, and the tools that they had put together. Skip put a half hitch around one of the pilings with the bow rope. The boat was beginning to settle on the sand as the tide was still receding. It was 9:30 in the morning and the mist was beginning to burn off of the water with the heat of the rising sun.

They started out across the half-mile stretch to the sea. Each boy took his load. The boys could not see the sand hill from where they had landed. So they walked across the sand dunes and scrub trees, skirted the pine forest, and came out on the beach. They walked up it until they could see the sand hill then went into the pine forest to where the chest was buried.

"There they go!" Burl said as he put down the binoculars.

The Rachel drifted quietly in the water about 1500 yards off shore.

"Well, let's make ourselves comfortable. Drop anchor!" Fin said.

Burl reached over and slung the anchor straight out from him. The line played out behind it until it sunk and dug into the shallow bottom. The Rachel shifted into the waves and they lop, lopped at her hull.

Fin took a long pull from a pint of whiskey then handed it over to Burl who wiped the lip of the bottle with the palm of his hand. The hazy sun was beginning to shine through the morning mist. It's going to be hot today, he thought as he looked off into the distance.

Scallop

Chapter 12

RECOVERING BLACKBEARD'S TREASURE

The boys reached the beach after about an hour's walk. It was hot now and their clothes were soaked through with sweat. The flies were all but gone now because they were away from the marshy area.

"Let's take a break!" Frankie said as they reached the beach crest.

Each boy dropped his burden and sat down, not saying anything at first, and looking out to sea. Frankie said excitedly, "Can't you just imagine a sailing ship off shore with a boat being rowed in with a treasure chest in it."

"I sure can. There are stories about treasures being buried on all of these islands," Sammy said.

They sat a while longer and then Skip said, "Let's go. It's already 10:30."

Each boy picked up his pack and they began to walk up the beach one behind the other. After half and hour Frankie stopped and pointed to the sand hill in the pines.

"It was about here that we went into the forest," Frankie said.

The boys now veered off of the hard beach sand and began the trek back across the soft white sand over the primary and secondary dunes, across the low sandy area and into the pines. They walked directly to the sand hill that was easily in view by now. Skip was the first to see the bone sticking out of the sand.

"There it is!" he said.

The boys gathered around and Frankie and Skip began to scrape sand away from the top of the chest. The top of the chest was now sticking above the sand.

"Let's use the shovels," Frankie said.

Skip and Frankie began to dig excitedly all around the chest until they had cleared a hole about six inches around each side.

"Let's try it now," Skip said.

Each boy dug his shovel under the chest and pried up at the same time. It hardly budged because of the vacuum created between the bottom of the chest and the moist sand. They tried again and this time the chest gave way with a sucking sound. Skip and Frankie grabbed a leather strap at one end of the chest and pulled while Sammy waited. The chest rose and tilted against the end of the hole. Sammy then jumped in and reached for the bottom of the chest.

"Yiiiii!" he yelled!

"What's wrong?" Skip said.

"Look!" he said, screwing up his nose.

Next to his left foot was a crushed skull with its eye sockets looking up at him.

"Come on! Let's get the chest out of the hole," Frankie said.

He and Skip pulled while Sammy lifted; and the chest was lifted up onto the ground. Skip took the hammer and smashed the lock. Sammy could see that two skeletons occupied the space now where the chest had been. Skip was not having much luck opening the lid.

"Let me try!" Frankie said.

He tried to insert a crowbar between the lid and the main body of the chest. It would not fit. By now it was getting hot and their tempers were getting short

"Give me that darned hammer!" Sammy said and Frankie gave it to him.

He walked around the chest then stopped. He suddenly smashed the hammer at a part of the chest made of wood. He struck again and again until he had broken through the wood and rusted iron. The biggest hole that he could make was about the size of a fifty-cent piece. He then got down on his knees and put his eye to the hole.

"What is it?" Frankie said. He didn't say anything for a while.

"What is it?" Frankie asked again excitedly.

"Look for yourself," Sammy said as he looked at each boy and grinned.

Each boy looked through the hole for a long time. Each pulled away from the hole saying,

"Gosh! Coins, gold coins is what I saw!" Skip said.

"That's what I saw too!" Each of the other two boys replied in unison.

"There must be a million dollars there!" Sammy said. The boys just stood there looking at the chest in disbelief.

"Gosh, I wonder where all this came from?" Skip said.

"Well, from what I can see what happened to these people, I sure hope that the owner doesn't come back to claim his property today. How are we going to get it back to the boat?" Frankie said.

"We'll have to carry the whole thing. We can't get into the chest with these tools," Skip said.

"We can take a short cut," Frankie said.

"That means that we will have to go near the marsh," Sammy said remembering the flies.

Sammy pointed to the bones in the hole.

" What about them?"

"Let's just cover them back up. Its too late for them now," Frankie said.

All three boys refilled the hole with sand after gathering up all of the bones and throwing them into the hole making it a common grave. The boys paused for a few minutes just because it seemed like the respectful thing to do. Skip and Frankie grabbed the two straps and Sammy lifted the back of the chest. They lifted as one and started off towards the boat. The boys had carried the chest about thirty yards and Skip had to stop. Each boy was gasping for breath and was sweating profusely. It took long hours to make the trip to the edge of the marsh in 10-20 yard charges of shifting arms and positions. They did anything to use different sets of muscles.

When they reached the marsh, they were about 300 yards from the boat. Those were the longest 300 yards they had ever run. The flies and mosquitoes were not only vicious but they were smart. They only bit the boys when they were running with the chest; and when they bit, it was as if they had three-inch teeth. They bit the boys only in places that they couldn't reach. Finally, the boys reached the hard beach sand and the boat. They collapsed on the crest of the beach with the chest. Skip lay across it. Sammy and Frankie lay on their backs on the soft white sand. Great whelts covered their arms and faces and they were burned lobster red from the sun. Their faces were beginning to swell.

" I didn't think that I was going to make the last ten yards," Skip gasped. Not one boy replied but Frankie did by barely raising his left hand.

The boys lay on the beach for half an hour. They drank hot water from the gallon jug that they had left in the bow of the boat. Hot water never tasted so good and they ate the cookies they brought with lunch. Gradually, they regained their strength and sat on the beach staring out at the bay. The Rachel swung at the anchor far away from shore. The boys did not seem to notice her because they were planning now how to load the chest into the boat.

Cutlas

Chapter 13

ABOARD THE RACHEL, ABOARD THE BOAT

Fin and Burl were groggy now. They both sat slumped in front of the wheelhouse propped up against it as they kept their eyes on the beach.

"There they are," Burl said looking through the binoculars as he had been doing ever so often for the last two hours.

"They've got a box of some kind," he said.

"Le me see," Fin said as he grabbed clumsily for the binoculars.

"They're loading the box into the boat," he said. He could see that the boys were struggling to lift the chest onto the bow. Two of them jumped into the boat and they lowered it into its center. The other larger boy got in and the three of them shifted the chest over the center seat slightly aft of amidships and over the keel.

"Must be something heavy in there," Fin said with a grin; and he looked at Burl who grinned lopsidedly back at him.

"We'll have to help them take it home," he said this time laughing aloud. "Go get the gun, Burl."

Burl went staggering off through the wheelhouse to the cabin below. A minute later, he came back up and joined Fin at the wheel in the cabin.

It was getting late now and the sun was getting low on the horizon. A hint of darkness was starting to creep onto the cove. The last of many fishermen who had stayed on late for one last bite had hoisted anchor and were heading for home. Only two boats now remained behind. It was 7:00 p.m. and a cool fog descended over the cove as the Rachel drifted and waited. Waited!

The three boys walked the boat away from shore out into the cove. The boat had proper trim and did not settle deep into the water. They gave one last shove and each boy jumped onto the rails and then assumed a position on each of the three seats. Frankie pushed the engine and the lower unit sank into the water. By now, the fog was settling bringing on darkness far sooner than they had anticipated. They could not see the Rachel for the fog in the distance hid her.

Doubloons

Dagger

Chapter 14

THE CHASE

Frankie could hear the fog horns in the cove; but he knew from experience that sound did strange things in a fog. It seemed to bounce around and come at you from all directions. It surrounded you just like the fog. But, he had a compass; and he was familiar with Toms Cove. The visibility was about a hundred yards; so they started home. Frankie cranked the engine twice and it caught on the third try. He moved the gearshift from neutral to forward and the boat began to lumber forward at a slow speed under its additional weight.

Fin had anticipated where the boys would have to pass the Rachel on their way home. He had moved her directly into their path. He could not believe how lucky he was that the fog had rolled in. Everyone else had left to go home; and it concealed the Rachel perfectly.

He could hear the boy's engine start; and he heard the boat coming his way. The water was as smooth as glass and the Rachel did not rock at all. The wind was at a calm. They were closer now. Burl strained to see them with the binoculars. Suddenly, he could see a dark form slowly emerging from the gray fog.

"Here they come!" he said excitedly in a whisper.

Fin could not see them clearly yet; nor could the boys see the Rachel. Then Fin saw them pass on by. He pressed the starter button with his thumb and the engine sputtered then caught. He pushed the throttle forward and the Rachel surged ahead settling at the stern. He started a course to gradually intersect their's about a few hundred yards ahead.

Skip was the first to see the trawler paralleling their course but getting larger all the while. It was big and black and eerie because it looked much larger than it really was in the fog. Skip looked back at Frankie and pointed to the bigger boat. Frankie gradually adjusted the steering so that the smaller boat's course began to parallel the trawler's course. He did not want to hit the trawler; nor did he want to have them come too close for inspection. The chest was in full view.

"They've seen us!" Burl said.

Just as he said that, Fin pushed the throttle forward and veered right heading directly for the little boat. He crossed behind her wake at the last minute and spun the wheel counterclockwise so that she was close and beside the boy's boat. Frankie saw the profile of the trawler change; and he surmised that it was heading directly for them.

"Hey!" he yelled. "Stop!" But before he could do anything the Rachel had passed astern and hove to right beside them.

Both boats were rocking and it was hard for Frankie to keep the little boat from being pulled by her wake under the wildly rocking Rachel. Burl was standing by the hole looking down at the boys. They saw that he had a pump shotgun; and he was pointing it at them. He motioned to Frankie with its tip and Frankie throttled back and the engine stopped. Fin cut his engines and both boats glided forward in parallel.

"Are you crazy, Burl?" screamed Sammy trying to bluff it through.

Burl said, "Shut up!"

Fin came back to Burl from the wheelhouse and told Skip to throw him the bowline. Skip did so and in a moment the rope was tied to a cleat. Gradually, the two boats bumped each other as they glided forward. The rocking had stopped considerably now.

Fin was shifting the boom now to a position over the little boat; and he pushed a switch and the cargo net slowly inched down. When it reached the boat he said, "Put the chest in the net boys."

Burl put even more emphasis on this by pressing the stock of the gun tighter into his shoulder. Each boy pulled a corner of the cargo net down until there was enough slack in the rope to allow it to lie flat on the bottom of the boat in front of the center seat. Frankie and Skip grabbed the two leather straps and Sammy lifted the other end. They lifted the chest over the center seat and onto the center of the cargo net.

The boys stepped back and without a word Fin started the winch and the cargo net began to rise. The sound of the winch lowered when the chest began to rise. Fin grabbed the net at the rail and swung the boom over the deck. He then reversed the winch and the chest was lowered gradually to the wooden deck beside Burl. It landed with a dull thud. He unhooked the net from the boom lines and centered the boom over the boat.

He then went forward and disappeared into the wheelhouse. He returned immediately with a red fire ax. He struck the chest with massive blows that echoed off into the distance. First, the iron began to break and then wood chips began to fly onto the deck and sprinkled the water. He was beating the chest apart. Burl had not budged an inch. Finally, the chest collapsed from the pounding and its centuries old secrets tumbled and jingled onto the deck. Fin's eyes widened; but the boys could not see the chest's contents for their eyes were below the level of the Rachel's rails.

"Gold coins! All of it. Thanks boys," he said. He winked at Burl. Burl grinned and took out his knife and cut the bowline tethered to the cleat. The little boat began to drift slowly away from the trawler.

"You'll never get away with this!" Frankie yelled shaking his fist.

"Never!" Skip said.

With that Burl pulled the trigger of the shotgun three times and blew three huge holes in the bottom the boy's boat. Fin waved at them over his shoulder as he walked back to the wheelhouse.

Just before he went inside, he turned and waved saying, "Bye! Bye!"

He then started the engine and pushed the throttle forward in gear and the Rachel gradually disappeared into the fog. The boys could hear the engines gradually fading off into the distance as the water began to rapidly fill the boat.

Shark

Chapter 15

THE EXPLOSION

"I guess that they want it to look like we drowned," Skip said.

"Stay with the boat," Sammy said. "It will float. Get everything with weight over the side."

Frankie unscrewed the engine from the transom while Sammy and Skip threw tools and gasoline and even the partially filled water jug overboard. Two of them lifted the engine and let it sink. The stern dipped at first and water poured into the boat; then the boat stabilized as the boys distributed their weight evenly over it. The boat gradually filled with water until the rails were even with the water's surface. They could not hear the Rachel's engines any more so they assumed that she had gone home. The three boys sat in water up to their shoulders. They were grateful that it was calm.

Fin cut the throttle back and the engine stopped. The Rachel glided forward. Burl had been sorting through the coins as he hunkered down onto the deck.

"My, we're rich," he said.

He reached into his shirt pocket for a cigarette, lit it, and threw the match over board. It extinguished with a hiss. Fin grinned as he hunkered down slowly and let the coins trickle through his fingers. They made a dull jingle as each one fell on top of the others. They were shiny in the subdued light and almost gleamed as they spread out in

a fan from the chest all over the deck for five feet around. And that was only a portion of the coins still within the chest.

He looked up at Burl and said, "We've got to go back."

"Why?" Burl said. "All they will find are dead bodies."

"It's wood. The boat will float," Fin said. "I forgot. We'll run them down."

Fin got up and walked back to the wheelhouse. He pressed the starter button and the engine turned over but only coughed smoke and did not catch. He tried again and again and again.

"Burl!" He yelled angrily as he leaned out of the wheelhouse. "Go see if the engine is flooded!!"

Burl raised the hatch to the engine room and started down the ladder. He could smell the gas. The Rachel exploded as his head went down the hatch. She blew up in three explosions. The first one acted as a primer for the second and third.

The engine room was filled with gas fumes that flashed into an explosion as Burl's head dipped below the level of the hatch cover. He had forgotten to throw away his cigarette amidst all of the excitement and confusion. The last thing that Burl saw was a bright flash. The last thing that he felt was numbness spreading over his body and darkness washing over him. The explosion tore up the wooden deck and broke through the steel 100-gallon gas tanks on each side behind the bulkhead in the stern. The second and third explosions tore the bottom out of the Rachel. The blue wheelhouse disappeared along with the decking. Coins were scattered everywhere at random and the chest was thrown a hundred yards away. Fin disappeared with the wheelhouse. The Rachel's gray hull burned as she settled hissing into the water. Her mast was blown away so she could not be seen from the surface. She hissed with steam rising from the water; and bubbles rose to the surface as she settled on the bottom. A small oily slick oozed from her. It was hardly noticeable from the surface.

The boys heard Fin trying to start the engines. They thought he had gone home.

"He's going to come back!" Skip said. "He knows this boat will float if all of the weight is taken off."

Then the engine stopped coughing and immediately they heard "KA POW! KA POW! KA POW! POW!" The explosions echoed in the fog.

They did not see the explosion because the fog enshrouded it; but they knew that it had happened. They did not know how or why it happened but they knew that the Rachel had blown up. It was quiet after that and the boys just sat in the boat. All that could be heard was the periodic tolling of the foghorn. No one talked because they were too cold. Late that evening, Frankie heard the sound of rushing water. He looked over and saw a fin slowly emerge from the water. It glided the length of the boat then submerged gracefully into the depths again. He didn't say anything to anyone hoping that it would go away. He never saw it again.

They shivered all night and into the next morning when the fog lifted with the morning sun. They could see a Coast Guard cutter, a 100 footer, in the distance coming towards them at full speed. They had been searching for the boys in the darkness. They had started at the mouth of the creek and worked their way back out to Toms Cove. Finally, they spotted the boys when the fog lifted. Rachel was nowhere to be seen.

The boys decided to tell their parents that they had hit a submerged log or the bottom or something on the way back in the fog. They did not see any reason to bring the treasure into it because it was gone. From now on they were not allowed to go out anymore in the boat without adults along.

Fin and Burl did not have any relatives so the island people were glad that they had gone. Some folks said that they had just moved on to another port. No one cared anyway. The boys didn't tell anyone what they knew. It would not have added much. They couldn't prove what happened anyway.

Frankie sat on the dock with his feet dangling in the water. It was hot and the blue sky was clear. He gazed off over the marsh towards the naval base. It was Thursday; and they probably wouldn't be flying.

What would he and Skip do today, he thought with a sigh? He got up and walked carefully back across the shells to the house.

Assateague Pony

EPILOGUE

Granddaddy was tired now. After all, it had been a rather exciting afternoon. Erin blinked and returned to reality. Allison waited for more. Granddaddy nudged Erin from his knee onto the floor and said, " I must rest my eyes now. I am tired." He then closed his eyes and drifted into a shallow, dreamlike sleep.

Allison and Erin went out to play.

HORSEFLIES, MOSQUITOES, AND GNATS, A POEM.

Horseflies, black and green,
    have a sense of smell very keen.
Life in the marsh is harsh my friend.
These flies prefer a sea blown wind
    with which to ride fast and bold
        in search of a feast about to unfold.

The back of the neck, the tops of the feet
    are delectable spots to ponder and seek.
First it lands and pats the meal
    rubbing its feet with gourmet zeal.
Then bracing its back against the wind
    it opens its mouth and just digs in.

Mosquitoes sing as they sample their wares.
It lightly wings it with very few cares.
It lands on the hand with indecision
    then shifts the feet before the final incision.

Gnats bother—they sing in the ears.
They fly up the nose and they pester the eye.
Last night a gnat sang busily in my ear.
"Hey," he said. "Do you hear?"

I lay there feigning a happy sleep.
He edged a bit closer, just a creep.
I opened one eye to the tiniest slit;
    and I raised my hand by a little bit.

He whined and he whined like a happy little fiddle;
    for he did not see the end of the riddle.
A little bit further and then, KER-SPLAT!
    and, that my friends was the end of that!

MEET THE AUTHOR

Frank, the author of *The Treasure of Assateague Island* - a Trafford best seller in 2005, grew up on the Eastern Shore of Virginia. Born in Northampton County in 1940, he was raised on Chincoteague Island during the late 1940s and early 1950s on the "gut", a narrows between Chincoteague Channel and Chincoteague Bay where he experienced many of the outdoor adventures of Frankie and Skip in the story. At the time the entire Eastern Shore was remote and isolated from the mainland, with no bridges or tunnels to connect to Virginia and Maryland's western shore. A bridge across to Assateague Island was not in existence at the time either.

In addition to his experiences and enjoyment of nature on Chincoteague and Assateague Islands, Frank saw the best of two worlds from his back door where the Chincoteague Naval Air Station was visible. The development of jet aircraft and rocketry at Wallops Island introduced him to the beauty and excitement of the world of science. Frank graduated from Atlantic High School (Arcadia) in 1958 and went on to a career as a professional biologist and life-long naturalist who has spoken and published at many zoological societies.

Oystering is a major industry on the Atlantic seacoast and the Chesapeake Bay of Maryland and Virginia. Harvesting oysters off their Northampton County seaside farm, Frank and his family enjoyed this delectable bounty for many years, but sadly, the oyster population is in danger. As a government scientist Frank participated in Chesapeake Bay oyster research. His newly released book for young children is a fantasy lesson in nature entitled Sandy and the Dancing Waves" in which Sandy, a young grain of sand, enjoys fun in the sun and through a series of adventures becomes a beautiful pearl. The story, revealing how a pearl is formed from a piece of sand and an oyster, is a very simple and delightful introduction to the wonders of natural science.

Frank is retired and lives in Maryland with his wife Therese. They have two married children Mary and John and three grandchildren. He enjoys his hobbies: wildlife biology, writing, painting, Senior Olympics, and travel.

Frankie, the author about ten years old, and his dog "Stinky" on the back porch of their Chincoteague home. Stinky is not in the story but he was a great part of Frankie's life on Chincoteague. He bought "Stinky" for two ice cream cones.

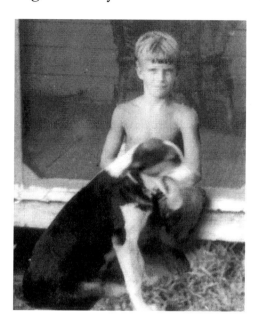

Frank on the docks in Chincoteague. He still enjoys the ships in the Channel and the barrier islands and wildlife.

ISBN 141205873-2

Made in the USA
Middletown, DE
13 April 2018